DATE DUE

APR 2 3 2008		
MAY 0 7 2008		
SEP 0 1 2010		
AUG 0 2 2011		
MAR 1 1 2017		

WITHDRAWN

D1449371

The Couch Was a Castle

Ruth Ohi

Annick Press
Toronto • New York • Vancouver

We acknowledge the support of the Canada Council for the Arts, the Ontario
Arts Council, and the Government of Canada through the Book Publishing
Industry Development Program (BPIDP) for our publishing activities.

Library and Archives Canada Cataloging in Publication

Ohi, Ruth
    The couch was a castle / written and illustrated by Ruth Ohi.

"A Ruth Ohi picture book".

ISBN-13: 978-1-55451-014-6 (bound)
ISBN-13: 978-1-55451-013-9 (pbk.).--
ISBN-10: 1-55451-014-7 (bound)
ISBN-10: 1-55451-013-9 (pbk.)

        I. Title.

PS8579.H47C69 2006   jC813'.6   C2006-901043-9

The art in this book was rendered in watercolor.
The text was typeset in ITC Mendoza Roman.

Distributed in Canada by: Published in the U.S.A. by:
Firefly Books Ltd.   Annick Press (U.S.) Ltd.
66 Leek Crescent   Distributed in the U.S.A. by:
Richmond Hill, ON   Firefly Books (U.S.) Inc.
L4B 1H1   P.O. Box 1338
                                 Ellicott Station
                                 Buffalo, NY 14205

Printed in China.

Visit us at: www.annickpress.com

This one's for Jim.
—R.O.

The couch was a castle –
a royal keep.

The couch was a horse –
gallop and leap.

The couch was for games
like hide-and-seek.

The couch was a boat
that sprung a leak.

The couch was a circus –
bounce and tumble.

The couch was a cave
starting to crumble.

The couch was a stage
for duels in the night.

The couch was a city
lost with fright.

The couch was quite lonely
when left with just one.

Isn't there someone
who'll rescue the fun?

The couch was for heroes,
for the very brave few.

The couch was a couch
for just me and you.